Are You

written by Pam Holden
illustrated by Kelvin Hawley

1

You get eggs
from the hens.

You get honey
from the bees.

Buzz, buzz.

You get apples
from the trees.

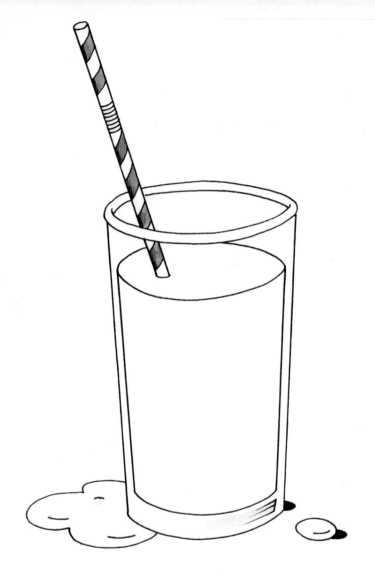

You get milk
from the cows.

9

You get juice
from the fruit.

You get fish
from the sea.

You get strawberries
from the garden.

You get ice cream
from the shop!